I0452465

TEXAS JOHN ALDEN

BY

ROBERT E. HOWARD

Copyright © 2013 Read Books Ltd.
This book is copyright and may not be
reproduced or copied in any way without
the express permission of the publisher in writing

British Library Cataloguing-in-Publication Data
A catalogue record for this book is available from the
British Library

Robert E. Howard

Robert Ervin Howard was born in Peaster, Texas in 1906. During his youth, his family moved between a variety of Texan boomtowns, and Howard – a bookish and somewhat introverted child – was steeped in the violent myths and legends of the Old South. Although he loved reading and learning, Howard developed a distinctly Texan, hardboiled outlook on the world. He became a passionate fan of boxing, taking it up at an amateur level, and from the age of nine began to write adventure tales of semi-historical bloodshed. In 1919, when Howard was thirteen, his family moved to the Central Texas hamlet of Cross Plains, where he would stay for the rest of his life.

At fifteen Howard began to read the pulp magazines of the day, and to write more seriously. The December 1922 issue of his high school newspaper featured two of his stories, 'Golden Hope Christmas' and 'West is West'. In 1924 he sold his first piece – a short caveman tale titled 'Spear and Fang' – for $16 to the not-yet-famous *Weird Tales* magazine. He published with the magazine regularly over the next few years. 1929 was a breakout year for Howard, in that the 23-year-old writer began to sell to other magazines, such as *Ghost Stories* and *Argosy*, both of whom had previously sent him hundreds of rejection slips. In 1930, he began a

1

correspondence with weird fiction master H. P. Lovecraft which ran up to his death six years later, and is regarded as one of the great correspondence cycles in all of fantasy literature.

It was partly due to Lovecraft's encouragement that Howard created his most famous character, Conan the Cimmerian. Conan – a barbarian-turned-King during the Hyborian Age, a mythical period of some 12,000 years ago – featured in seventeen *Weird Tales* stories between 1933 and 1936, and is now regarded as having spawned the 'sword and sorcery' genre, making Howard's influence on fantasy literature comparable to that of J. R. R. Tolkien's. The Conan stories have since been adapted many times, most famously in the series of films starring Arnold Schwarzenegger.

Howard was enjoying an all-time high in sales by the beginning of 1936, but he was also deeply upset by the ill health of his mother, who had fallen into a coma. On the morning of June 11, 1936, he asked an attending nurse whether she would ever recover, and the nurse replied negatively. Howard walked to his car, parked outside the family home in Cross Plains, and shot himself. He died eight hours later, aged just thirty.

I hear the citizens of War Whoop has organized theirselves into a committee of public safety which they says is to pertect the town agen me, Breckinridge Elkins. Sech doings as that irritates me. You'd think I was a public menace or something.

I'm purty dern tired of their slanders. I didn't tear down their cussed jail; the buffalo-hunters done it. How could I when I was in it at the time?

As for the Silver Boot saloon and dance hall, it wouldn't of got shot up if the owner had showed any sense. It was Ace Middleton's own fault he got his hind laig busted in three places, and if the city marshal had been tending to his own business instead of persecuting a pore, helpless stranger, he wouldn't of got the seat of his britches full of buckshot.

Folks which says I went to War Whoop a-purpose to wreck the town, is liars. I never had no idea at first of going there at all. It's off the railroad and infested with tinhorn gamblers and buffalo-hunters and sech-like varmints, and no place for a trail-driver.

My visit to this lair of vice come about like this: I'd rode p'int on a herd of longhorns clean from the lower Pecos to Goshen, where the railroad was. And I stayed there after the trail-boss and the other boys headed south, to spark the belle of the town, Betty Wilkinson, which gal was as purty as a brand-new bowie knife. She seemed to like me middling

3

tolerable, but I had rivals, notably a snub-nosed Arizona waddy by the name of Bizz Ridgeway.

This varmint's persistence was so plumb aggravating that I come in on him sudden-like one morning in the back room of the Spanish Mustang, in Goshen, and I says:

"Lissen here, you sand-burr in the pants of progress, I'm a peaceable man, generous and retirin' to a fault. But I'm reachin' the limit of my endurance. Ain't they no gals in Arizona, that you got to come pesterin' mine? Whyn't yuh go on back home where you belong anyhow? I'm askin' yuh like a gent to keep away from Betty Wilkinson before somethin' onpleasant is forced to happen to yuh."

He kind of r'ared up, and says: "I ain't the only gent which is sparkin' Betty. Why don't you make war-talk to Rudwell Shapley, Jr.?"

"He ain't nothin' but a puddin'-headed tenderfoot," I responded coldly. "I don't consider him in no serious light. A gal with as much sense as Betty wouldn't pay him no mind. But you got a slick tongue and might snake yore way ahead of me. So I'm tellin' you--"

He started to git up in a hurry, and I reached for my bowie, but then he sunk back down in his chair and to my amazement he busted into tears.

"What in thunder's the matter with you?" I demanded, shocked.

"Woe is me!" moaned he. "Yuh're right, Breck. I got no business hangin' around Betty. But I didn't know she was yore gal. I ain't got no matrimonial intentions onto her. I'm jest kind of consolin' myself with her company, whilst bein' parted by crooel Fate from my own true love."

"Hey," I says, pricking up my ears and uncocking my pistol. "You ain't in love with Betty? You got another gal?"

"A pitcher of divine beauty!" vowed he, wiping his eyes on my bandanner. "Gloria La Venner, which sings in the Silver Boot, over to War Whoop. We was to wed--"

Here his emotions overcome him and he sobbed loudly.

"But Fate interfered," he moaned. "I was banished from War Whoop, never to return. In a thoughtless moment I kind of pushed a bartender with a clawhammer, and he had a stroke of apperplexity or somethin' and died, and they blamed me. I was forced to flee without tellin' my true love where I was goin'.

"I ain't dared to go back because them folks over there is so prejudiced agen' me they threatens to arrest me on sight. My true love is eatin' her heart out, waitin' for me to come and claim her as my bride, whilst I lives here in exile!"

Bizz then wept bitterly on my shoulder till I throwed him off in some embarrassment.

"Whyn't yuh write her a letter, yuh dad-blamed fool?" I ast.

"I can't write, nor read, neither," he said. "And I don't trust nobody to send word to her by. She's so beautiful, the critter I'd send would probably fall in love with her hisself, the lowdown polecat!" Suddenly he grabbed my hand with both of his'n, and said, "Breck, you got a honest face, and I never did believe all they say about you, anyway. Why'n't you go and tell her?"

"I'll do better'n that if it'll keep you away from Betty," I says. "I'll bring this gal over here to Goshen."

"Yuh're a gent!" says he, wringing my hand. "I wouldn't entrust nobody else with sech a sacred mission. Jest go to the Silver Boot and tell Ace Middleton you want to see Gloria La Venner alone."

"All right," I said. "I'll rent a buckboard to bring her back in."

"I'll be countin' the hours till yuh heaves over the horizen with my true love!" declaimed he, reaching for the whiskey bottle.

So I hustled out, and who should I run into but that pore sapified shrimp of a Rudwell Shapley Joonyer in his monkey jacket and tight riding pants and varnished English boots. We like to had a collision as I barged through the swinging doors and he squeaked and staggered back and hollered: "Don't shoot!"

"Who said anything about shootin'?" I ast irritably, and he kind of got his color back and looked me over like I was a sideshow or something, like he always done.

"Your home," says he, "is a long way from here, is it not, Mister Elkins?"

"Yeah," I said. "I live on Wolf Mountain, 'way down near whar the Pecos runs into the Rio Grande."

"Indeed!" he says kind of hopefully. "I suppose you'll be returning soon?"

"Naw, I ain't," I says. "I'll probably stay here all fall."

"Oh!" says he dejectedly, and went off looking like somebody had kicked him in the pants. I wondered why he should git so down-in-the-mouth jest because I warn't goin' home. But them tenderfoots ain't got no sense and they ain't no use wasting time trying to figger out why they does things, because they don't generally know theirselves.

For instance, why should a object like Rudwell Shapley Jr. come to Goshen, I want to know? I ast him once p'int blank and he says it was a primitive urge so see life in the raw, whatever that means. I thought maybe he was talking about grub, but the cook at the Laramie Restaurant said he takes his beefsteaks well done like the rest of us.

Well, anyway, I got onto my hoss Cap'n Kidd and pulled for War Whoop which laid some miles west of Goshen. I warn't wasting no time, because the quicker I got Gloria La Venner to Goshen, the quicker I'd have a clear field with

Betty. Of course it would of been easier and quicker jest to shoot Bizz, but I didn't know how Betty'd take it. Women is funny that way.

I figgered to eat dinner at the Half-Way House, a tavern which stood on the prairie about half-way betwix Goshen and War Whoop, but as I approached it I met a most pecooliar-looking object heading east.

I presently recognized it as a cowboy name Tump Garrison, and he looked like he'd been through a sorghum mill. His hat brim was pulled loose from the crown and hung around his neck like a collar, his clothes hung in rags. His face was skint all over, and one ear showed signs of having been chawed on long and earnestly.

"Where was the tornado?" I ast, pulling up.

He give me a suspicious look out of the eye he could still see with.

"Oh, it's you Breck," he says then. "My brains is so addled, I didn't recognize you at first. In fact," says he, tenderly caressing a lump on his head the size of a turkey aig, "It's jest a few minutes ago that I managed to remember my own name."

"What happened?" I ast with interest.

"I ain't shore," says he, spitting out three or four loose tushes. "Leastways I ain't shore jest what happened after that there table laig was shattered over my head. Things is a little foggy after that. But up to that time my memory is flawless.

"Briefly, Breck," says he, rising in his stirrups to rub his pants where they was the print of a boot heel, "I diskivered that I warn't welcome at the Half-Way House, and big as you be, I advises yuh to avoid it like yuh would the yaller j'indus."

"It's a public tavern," I says.

"It was," says he, working his right laig to see if it was still in j'int. "It was till Moose Harrison, the buffalo-hunter, arrove there to hold a private celebration of his own. He don't like cattle nor them which handles 'em. He told me so hisself, jest before he hit me with the bung-starter.

"He said he warn't aimin' to be pestered by no dern Texas cattle-pushers whilst he's enjoyin' a little relaxation. It was jest after issuin' this statement that he throwed me through the roulette wheel."

"You ain't from Texas," I said. "Yuh're from the Nations."

"That's what I told him whilst he was doin' a war-dance on my brisket," says Tump. "But he said he was too broadminded to bother with technicalities. Anyway, he says cowboys was the plague of the range, irregardless of where they come from."

"Oh, he did, did he?" I says irritably. "Well, I ain't huntin' trouble. I'm on a errand of mercy. But he better not shoot off his big mouth to me. I eats my dinner at the Half-Way House, regardless of all the buffler-hunters north of the Cimarron."

"I'd give a dollar to see the fun," says Tump. "But my other eye is closin' fast and I got to git amongst friends."

So he pulled for Goshen and I rode on to the Half-Way House, where I seen a big bay hoss tied to the hitch-rack. I watered Cap'n Kidd and went in. "Hssss!" the bartender says. "Git out as quick as yuh can! Moose Harrison's asleep in the back room!"

"I'm hongry," I responded, setting down at a table which stood nigh the bar. "Bring me a steak with pertaters and onions and a quart of coffee and a can of cling peaches. And whilst the stuff's cookin' gimme nine or ten bottles of beer to wash the dust out of my gullet."

"Lissen!" says the barkeep. "Reflect and consider. Yuh're young and life is sweet. Don't yuh know that Moose Harrison is pizen to anything that looks like a cowpuncher? When he's on a whiskey-tear, as at present, he's more painter than human. He's kilt more men--"

"Will yuh stop blattin' and bring me my rations?" I requested.

He shakes his head sad-like and says: "Well, all right. After all, it's yore hide. At least, try not to make no racket. He's swore to have the life blood of anybody which wakes him up."

I said I didn't want no trouble with nobody, and he tiptoed back to the kitchen and whispered my order to the cook, and then brung me nine or ten bottles of beer and slipped back behind the bar and watched me with morbid fascination.

I drunk the beer and whilst drinking I got to kind of brooding about Moose Harrison having the nerve to order everybody to keep quiet whilst he slept. But they're liars which claims I throwed the empty bottles at the door of the back room a-purpose to wake Harrison up.

When the waiter brung my grub I wanted to clear the table to make room for it, so I jest kind of tossed the bottles aside, and could I help it if they all busted on the back-room door? Was it my fault that Harrison was sech a light sleeper?

But the bartender moaned and ducked down behind the bar, and the waiter run through the kitchen and follered the cook in a sprint acrost the prairie, and a most remarkable beller burst forth from the back room.

The next instant the door was tore off the hinges and a enormous human come bulging into the barroom. He wore buckskins, his whiskers bristled, and his eyes was red as a drunk Comanche's.

"What in tarnation?" remarked he in a voice which cracked the winder panes. "Does my gol-blasted eyes deceive me? Is that there a cussed cowpuncher settin' there wolfin' beefsteak as brash as if he was a white man?"

"You ride herd on them insults!" I roared, rising sudden, and his eyes kind of popped when he seen I was about three inches taller'n him. "I got as much right here as you have."

"Name yore weppins," blustered he. He had a butcher knife and two six-shooters in his belt.

"Name 'em yoreself," I snorted. "If you thinks yuh're sech a hell-whizzer at fist-and-skull, why, shuck yore weppin-belt and I'll claw yore ears off with my bare hands!"

"That suits me!" says he. "I'll festoon that bar with yore innards," and he takes hold of his belt like he was going to unbuckle it--then, quick as a flash, he whipped out a gun. But I was watching for that and my right-hand .45 banged jest as his muzzle cleared leather.

The barkeep stuck his head up from behind the bar.

"Heck," he says wild-eyed, "you beat Moose Harrison to the draw, and him with the aidge! I wouldn't of believed it was possible if I hadn't saw it! But his friends will ride yore trail for this!"

"Warn't it self-defence?" I demanded.

"A clear case," says he. "But that won't mean nothin' to them wild and woolly buffalo-skinners. You better git back to Goshen where yuh got friends."

"I got business in War Whoop," I says. "Dang it, my coffee's cold. Dispose of the carcass and heat it up, will yuh?"

So he drug Harrison out, cussing because he was so heavy, and claiming I ought to help him. But I told him it warn't my tavern, and I also refused to pay for a decanter which Harrison's wild shot had busted. He got mad and said he hoped the buffalo-hunters did hang me. But I told him they'd have to ketch me without my guns first, and I slept with them on.

Then I finished my dinner and pulled for War Whoop.

It was about sundown when I got there, and I was purty hongry again. But I aimed to see Bizz's gal before I done anything else. So I put my hoss in the livery stable and seen he had a big feed, and then I headed for the Silver Boot, which was the biggest j'int in town.

There was plenty hilarity going on, but I seen no cowboys. The revelers was mostly gamblers, or buffalo-hunters, or soldiers, or freighters. War Whoop warn't popular with cattlemen. They warn't no buyers nor loading pens there, and for pleasure it warn't nigh as good a town as Goshen, anyway. I ast a barman where Ace Middleton was, and he p'inted out a big feller with a generous tummy decorated with a fancy vest and a gold watch chain about the size of a trace chain. He wore mighty handsome clothes and a diamond hoss-shoe stick pin and waxed mustache.

So I went up to him. He looked me over with very little favor.

"Oh, a cowpuncher, eh? Well, your money's as good as anybody's. Enjoy yourself, but don't get wild."

"I ain't aimin' to git wild," I says. "I want to see Gloria La Venner."

When I says that, he give a convulsive start and choked on his cigar. Everybody nigh us stopped laughing and talking and turned to watch us.

"What did you say?" he gurgled, gagging up the cigar. "Did I honestly hear you asking to see Gloria La Venner?"

"Shore," I says. "I aim to take her back to Goshen to git married--"

"You $&*!" says he, and grabbed up a table, broke off a laig and hit me over the head with it. It was most unexpected and took me plumb off guard.

I hadn't no idee what he was busting the table up for, and I was too surprised to duck. If it hadn't been for my Stetson it might of cracked my head. As it was, it knocked me back into the crowd, but before I could git my balance three or four bouncers grabbed me and somebody jerked my pistol out of the scabbard.

"Throw him out!" roared Ace, acting like a wild man. He was plumb purple in the face. "Steal my girl, will he? Hold him while I bust him in the snoot!"

He then rushed up and hit me very severely in the nose, whilst them bouncers was holding my arms. Well, up to that time I hadn't made no resistance. I was too astonished. But this was going too far, even if Ace was loco, as it appeared.

Nobody warn't holding my laigs, so I kicked Ace in the stummick and he curled up on the floor with a strangled shriek. I then started spurring them bouncers in the laigs and they yelled and let go of me, and somebody hit me in the ear with a blackjack.

That made me mad, so I reched for my bowie in my boot, but a big red-headed maverick kicked me in the face when I stooped down. That straightened me up, so I hit him on the jaw and he fell down acrost Ace which was holding his stummick and trying to yell for the city marshal.

Some low-minded scoundrel got a strangle-holt around my neck from behind and started beating me on the head with a pair of brass knucks. I ducked and throwed him over my head. Then I kicked out backwards and knocked over a couple more. But a scar-faced thug with a baseball bat got in a full-armed lick about that time and I went to my knees feeling like my skull was dislocated.

Six or seven of them then throwed theirselves onto me with howls of joy, and I seen I'd have to use vi'lence in spite of myself. So I drawed my bowie and started cutting my way through 'em. They couldn't of let go of me quicker if I'd been a cougar. They scattered every which-a-way, spattering blood and howling blue murder, and I riz r'aring and rampacious.

Somebody shot at me jest then, and I wheeled to locate him when a man run in at the door and p'inted a pistol at me. Before I could sling my knife through him, which was my earnest intention, he hollered:

"Drap yore deadly weppin! I'm the city marshal and yuh're under arrest!"

"What for?" I demanded. "I ain't done nothing."

"Nothing!" says Ace Middleton fiercely, as his menials lifted him onto his feet. "You've just sliced pieces out of five or six of our leading citizens! And there's my head bouncer, Red Croghan, out cold with a busted jaw. To say nothing of pushing my stomach through my spine. Ow! You must have mule blood in you, blast your soul!"

"Santry," he ordered the marshal, "he came in here drunk and raging and threatening, and started a fight for nothing. Do your duty! Arrest the cussed outlaw!"

Well, pap always tells me not to never resist no officer of the law, and anyway the marshal had my gun, and so many people was hollering and cussing and talking it kind of confused me. When they's any thinking to be did, I like to have a quiet place to do it and plenty of time.

So the first thing I knowed Santry had handcuffs on me and he hauls me off down the street with a big crowd follering and making remarks which is supposed to be funny.

They come to a log hut with bars on the back winder, take off the handcuffs, shove me in and lock the door. There I was in jail without even seeing Gloria La Venner. It was plumb disgustful.

The crowd all hustled back to the Silver Boot to watch them fellers git sewed up which had fell afoul of my bowie, all but one fat cuss which said he was a guard, and he sot down in front of the jail with a double-barreled shotgun acrost his lap and went to sleep.

Well, there warn't nothing in the jail but a bunk with a hoss blanket on it, and a wooden bench. The bunk was too short for me to sleep on with any comfort, being built for a six foot man, so I sot down on it and waited for somebody to bring me some grub.

So after a while the marshal come and looked in at the winder and cussed me.

"It's a good thing for you," he says, "that yuh didn't kill none of them fellers. As it is, maybe we won't hang yuh."

"Yuh won't have to hang me if yuh don't bring me some grub purty soon," I said. "Are yuh goin' to let me starve in this dern jail?"

"We don't encourage crime in our town by feedin' criminals," he says. "If yuh want grub, gimme the money to buy it with."

I told him I didn't have but five bucks and I thought I'd pay my fine with that. He said five bucks wouldn't begin to pay my fine, so I gave him the five-spot to buy grub with, and he took it and went off.

I waited and waited, and he didn't come. I hollered to the guard, but he kept on snoring. Then purty soon somebody said: "Psst!" at the winder. I went over and looked out, and they was a woman standing behind the jail. The moon had come up over the prairie as bright as day, and though she had a cloak with a hood throwed over her, by what I could see of her face she was awful purty.

"I'm Gloria La Venner," says she. "I'm risking my life coming here, but I wanted to get a look at the man who was crazy enough to tell Ace Middleton he wanted to see me."

"What's crazy about that?" I ast.

"Don't you know Ace has killed three men already for trying to flirt with me?" says she. "Any man who can break Red Croghan's jaw like you did must be a bear-cat--but it was sheer madness to tell Ace you wanted to marry me."

"Aw, he never give me time to explain about that," I says. "It warn't me which wants to marry yuh. But what business is it of Middleton's? This here's a free country."

"That's what I thought till I started working for him," she says bitterly. "He fell in love with me, and he's so insanely jealous he won't let anybody even speak to me. He keeps me practically a prisoner and watches me like a hawk. I can't get away from him. Nobody in town dares to help me. They won't even rent me a horse at the livery stable.

"You see Ace owns most of the town, and lots of people are in debt to him. The rest are afraid of him. I guess I'll have to spend the rest of my life under his thumb," she says despairfully.

"Yuh won't, neither," I says. "As soon as I can git word to my friends in Goshen to send me a loan to pay my fine and git me out of this fool jail, I'll take yuh to Goshen where yore true love is pinin' for yuh."

"My true love?" says she, kind of startled-like. "What do you mean?"

"Bizz Ridgeway is in Goshen," I says. "He don't dare come after yuh hisself, so he sent me to fetch yuh."

She didn't say nothing for a spell, and then she spoke kind of breathless.

"All right, I must get back to the Silver Boot now, or Ace will miss me and start looking for me. I'll find Santry and pay your fine tonight. When he lets you out, come to the back door of the Silver Boot and wait in the alley. I'll come to you there as soon as I can slip away."

So I said all right, and she went away. The guard setting in front of the jail with his shotgun acrost his knees hadn't never woke up. But he did wake up about fifteen minutes after she left. A gang of men came up the street, whooping and cussing, and he jumped to his feet.

"Curses! Here comes Brant Hanson and a mob of them buffler-hunters, and they got a rope! They're headin' for the jail!"

"Who do yuh reckon they're after?" I inquired.

"They ain't nobody in jail but you," he suggested p'intedly. "And in about a minute they ain't goin' to be nobody nigh it but you and them. When Hanson and his bunch is in licker they don't care who they shoots!"

He then laid down his shotgun and lit a shuck down a back alley as hard as he could leg it.

So about a dozen buffalo-hunters in buckskins and whiskers come surging up to the jail and kicked on the door. They couldn't get the door open so they went around behind the shack and looked in at the winder.

"It's him, all right," said one of 'em. "Let's shoot him through the winder."

But the others said, "Naw, let's do the job in proper order," and I ast them what they wanted.

"We aims to hang yuh!" they answered enthusiastically.

"You cain't do that," I says. "It's agen the law."

"You kilt Moose Harrison!" said the biggest one, which they called Hanson.

"Well, it was a even break, and he tried to git the drop on me," I says.

Then Hanson says: "Enough of sech quibblin'. We made up our mind to hang yuh, so le's don't hear no more argyments about it. Here," he says to his pals, "tie a rope to the bars and we'll jerk the whole winder out. It'll be easier'n bustin' down the door. And hustle up, because I'm in a hurry to git back to that poker game in the R'arin' Buffalo."

So they tied a rope onto the bars and all laid onto it and heaved and grunted, and some of the bars come loose at one end. I picked up the bench aiming to bust their fool skulls with it as they clumb through the winder, but jest then another feller run up.

"Wait, boys," he hollered, "don't waste yore muscle. I jest seen Santry down at the Topeka Queen gamblin' with the money he taken off that dern cowboy, and he gimme the key to the door."

So they abandoned the winder and surged arount to the front of the jail, and I quick propped the bench agen the door, and run to the winder and tore out them bars which was already loose. I could hear 'em rattling at the door, and as I clumb through the winder one of 'em said: "The lock's turned but the door's stuck. Heave agen it."

So whilst they hev I run around the jail and picks up the guard's shotgun where he'd dropped it when he run off. Jest then the bench inside give way and the door flew open, and all them fellers tried to crowd through. As a result they was all jammed in the door and cussin' something fierce.

21

"Quit crowdin'," yelled Hanson. "Holy catamount, he's gone! The jail's empty!"

I then up with my shotgun and give 'em both barrels in the seat of their britches, which was the handiest to aim at, and they let out a most amazing squall and busted loose and fell headfirst into the jail. Some of 'em kept on going head-down like they'd started and hit the back wall so hard it knocked 'em stiff, and the others fell over 'em.

They was all tangled in a pile cussing and yelling to beat the devil, so I slammed the door and locked it and run around behind the jail house. Hanson was trying to climb out the winder, so I hit him over the head with my shotgun and he fell back inside and hollered.

"Halp! I'm mortally injured!"

"Shet up that unseemly clamor," I says sternly. "Ain't none of yuh hurt bad. Throw yore guns out the winder and lay down on the floor. Hustle, before I gives you another blast through the winder."

They didn't know the shotgun was empty, so they throwed their weppins out in a hurry and laid down, but they warn't quiet about it. They seemed to consider they'd been subjected to crooel and onusual treatment, and the birdshot in their sterns must of been a-stinging right smart, because the language they used was plumb painful to hear. I stuck a couple of their pistols in my belt.

"If one of you shows his head at that winder within a hour," I said, "he'll git it blowed off."

I then snuck back into the shadders and headed for the livery stable.

The livery stable man was reading a newspaper by a lantern, and he looked surprised and said he thought I was in jail. I ignored this remark, and told him to hitch me a fast hoss to a buckboard whilst I saddled Cap'n Kidd.

"Wait a minute!" says he. "I hear tell yuh told Ace Middleton yuh aimed to elope with Gloria La Venner. Yuh takin' this rig for her?"

"Yes, I am," I says.

"Well I'm a friend of Middleton's," he says, "and I won't rent yuh no rig under no circumstances."

"Then git outa my way," I said. "I'll hitch the hoss up myself."

He then drawed a bowie so I clinched with him, and as we was rasseling around he sort of knocked his head agen a swingletree I happen to have in my hand at the time, and collapses with a low gurgle. So I tied him up and rolled him under a oats bin. I also rolled out a buckboard and hitched the best-looking harness hoss I could find to it, but them folks is liars which is going around saying I stole that there outfit. It was sent back later.

I saddles my hoss and tied him on behind the buckboard and got in and started for the Silver Boot, wondering how long it would take them fool buffalo-hunters to find out I was jest bluffing, and warn't lying out behind the jail to shoot 'em as they climb out.

I turnt into the alley which run behind the Silver Boot and then tied the hosses and went up to the back door and peeked in. Gloria was there. She grabbed me and I could feel her trembling.

"I thought you'd never come!" she whispered. "It'll be time for my singing-act again in just a few minutes. I've been waiting here ever since I paid Santry your fine. What kept you so long? He left the Silver Boot as soon as I gave him the money."

"He never turned me out, the low-down skunk," I muttered. "Some--er--friends got me out. Come on, git in the buckboard."

I helped her up and gave her the lines.

"I got a debt to settle before I leave town," I said. "You go on and wait for me at that clump of cottonwoods east of town. I'll be on purty soon."

So she pulled out in a hurry and I got onto Cap'n Kidd. I rode him around to the front of the Silver Boot, tied him to the hitch-rack and dismounted. The Silver Boot was crowded. I could see Ace strutting around chawing a big black cigar, and joking and slapping folks on the back.

Everybody was having sech a hilarious time nobody noticed me as I stood in the doorway, so I pulled the buffalo-hunters' .45's, and let bam at the mirror behind the bar. The barman yelped and ducked the flying glass, and everybody whirled and gaped, and Ace jerked his cigar out of his mouth and bawled:

"It's that dern cowpuncher again! Get him!"

But them bouncers had seen my guns, and they was shying away, all except the scar-faced thug which had hit me with the bat, and he whipped a gun from under his vest. So I shot him through the right shoulder, and he fell over behind the monte table.

I begun to spray the crowd with hot lead free and generous and they stampeded every which-a-way. Some went through the winder, glass and all, and some went out the side doors, and some busted down the back door in their flight.

I likewise riddled the mirror behind the bar and shot down some of the hanging lamps and busted most of the bottles on the shelves.

Ace ducked behind a stack of beer kaigs and opened fire on me, but he showed pore judgement in not noticing he was right under a hanging lamp. I shot if off the ceiling and it fell down on his head, and you ought to of heard him holler when the burning ile run down his wuthless neck.

He come prancing into the open, wiping his neck with one hand and trying to shoot me with the other'n, and I

25

drilled him through the hind laig. He fell down and bellered like a bull with its tail cotched in a fence gate.

"You dern murderer!" says he passionately. "I'll have yore life for this!"

"Shet up!" I snarled. "I'm jest payin' yuh back for all the pain and humiliation I suffered in this den of iniquity--"

At this moment a bartender riz up from behind a billiard table with a sawed-off shotgun, but I shot it out of his hands before he could cock it, and he fell over backwards hollering: "Spare my life!" Jest then somebody yelled: "Halt, in the name of the law!" and I looked around and it was that tinhorn marshal named Santry with a gun in his hand.

"I arrests you again!" he bawled. "Lay down yore weppins!"

"I'll lay yore carcase down," I responded. "Yuh ain't fitten for to be no law-officer. Yuh gambled away the five dollars I give yuh for grub, and yuh took the fine-money Miss La Venner give yuh, and didn't turn me out, and yuh give the key to them mobsters which wanted to hang me. You ain't no law. Yuh're a dern outlaw yoreself. Now yuh got a gun in yore hand same as me. Either start shootin' or throw it down!"

Well, he hollered, "Don't shoot!" and throwed it down and h'isted his hands. I seen he had my knife and pistol stuck in his belt, so I took them off of him, and tossed the

.45's I'd been using onto the billiard table and said, "Give these back to the buffalo-hunters."

But jest then he whipped out a .38 he was wearing under his arm, and shot at me and knocked my hat off, and then he turnt and run around the end of the bar, all bent over to git his head below it. So I grabbed the bartender's shotgun and let bam with both barrels jest as his rear end was going out of sight.

He shrieked blue ruin and started having a fit behind the bar, so I throwed the shotgun through the roulette wheel and stalked forth, leaving Ace and the bouncer and the marshal wailing and wallering on the floor. It was plumb disgustful the way they wept and cussed over their trifling injuries.

I come out on the street so sudden that them cusses which was hiding behind the hoss trough to shoot me as I come out, was took by surprise and only grazed me in a few places, so I throwed a few slugs amongst 'em and they took to their heels.

I got on Cap'n Kidd and headed east down the street, ignoring the shots fired at me from the alleys and winders. That is, I ignored 'em except to shoot back at 'em as I run, and I reckon that's how the mayor got the lobe of his ear shot off. I thought I heard somebody holler when I answered a shot fired at me from behind the mayor's board fence.

Well, when I got to the clump of cottonwoods there warn't no sign of Gloria, the hoss, or the buckboard, but there was a note stuck up on a tree which I grabbed and read by the light of the moon.

It said:

Dear Tejano:

Your friend must have been kidding you. I never even knew anybody named Bizz Ridgeway. But I'm taking this chance of getting away from Ace. I'm heading for Trevano Springs, and I'll send back the buckboard from there. Thank you for everything.

Gloria La Venner.

I got to Goshen about sunup, having loped all the way. Bizz Ridgeway was at the bar of the Spanish Mustang, and when he seen me he turned pale and dived for the winder, but I grabbed him.

"What you mean by tellin' me that lie about you and Gloria La Venner?" I demanded wrathfully. "Was you tryin' to git me kilt?"

"Well," says he, "to tell the truth, Breck, I was. All's fair in love or war, yuh know. I wanted to git yuh out of the way so I'd have a clear field with Betty Wilkinson, and I knowed about Ace Middleton and Gloria, and figgered he'd do the job if I sent yuh over there. But yuh needn't git mad. It didn't do me no good. Betty's already married."

"What?" I yelled.

He ducked instinctively.

"Yeah!" he says. "He took advantage of yore absence to pop the question, and she accepted him, and they're on their way to Kansas City for their honeymoon. He never had the nerve to ast her when you was in town, for fear yuh'd shoot him. They're goin' to live in the East because he's too scairt of you to come back."

"Who?" I screamed, foaming slightly at the mouth.

"Rudwell Shapley Jr.," says he. "It's all yore fault--"

It was at this moment that I dislocated Bizz Ridgeway's hind laig. I likewise defies the criticism which has been directed at this perfectly natural action. A Elkins with a busted heart is no man to trifle with.

www.ingramcontent.com/pod-product-compliance
Lightning Source LLC
Chambersburg PA
CBHW030243180626
46810CB00008B/3267